This Book has been donated to
your library by

The American Association
of
University Women

of North  Carolina.

It received the 2013 North Carolina
Juvenile Literature Award.

**AAUW**

**empowering women since 1881**

# Tea Cakes for Tosh

Kelly Starling Lyons ✦ *Illustrated by* E. B. Lewis

G. P. Putnam's Sons

An Imprint of Penguin Group (USA) Inc.

G. P. Putnam's Sons
A division of Penguin Young Readers Group.
Published by The Penguin Group.
Penguin Group (USA) Inc., 375 Hudson Street, New York, NY 10014, U.S.A.
Penguin Group (Canada), 90 Eglinton Avenue East, Suite 700, Toronto, Ontario
M4P 2Y3, Canada (a division of Pearson Penguin Canada Inc.).
Penguin Books Ltd, 80 Strand, London WC2R 0RL, England.
Penguin Ireland, 25 St. Stephen's Green, Dublin 2, Ireland (a division of Penguin Books Ltd.).
Penguin Group (Australia), 250 Camberwell Road, Camberwell, Victoria 3124,
Australia (a division of Pearson Australia Group Pty Ltd).
Penguin Books India Pvt Ltd, 11 Community Centre,
Panchsheel Park, New Delhi - 110 017, India.
Penguin Group (NZ), 67 Apollo Drive, Rosedale, Auckland 0632,
New Zealand (a division of Pearson New Zealand Ltd.).
Penguin Books (South Africa) (Pty) Ltd, 24 Sturdee Avenue,
Rosebank, Johannesburg 2196, South Africa.
Penguin Books Ltd, Registered Offices: 80 Strand, London WC2R 0RL, England.

Design by Annie Ericsson. Text set in Italian Old Style MT Std.
Library of Congress Cataloging-in-Publication Data is available upon request.

ISBN 978-0-399-25213-6
3 5 7 9 10 8 6 4 2

*For my grandmother, Ruth Woods Starling,*

*whose stories sent me from her Pittsburgh kitchen to another time.*

*And for my mother, Deborah Starling-Pollard,*

*who gave me wings.*

—KSL


*To Bernadette Trajano.*

—EBL

Tosh loved when his grandma Honey baked her golden tea cakes. The cookies smelled like vanilla mixed with sunshine. The taste warmed his heart, just like Honey's stories of courage did.

"Long ago, before you and I were born," Honey always began, "our people were enslaved."

In a blink, her words carried him to another place and time. Tosh saw tiny clouds of white dotting an endless field. He saw people picking cotton, heard their prayerful songs. In the plantation kitchen, he saw sweat running down a woman's face.

"Your great-great-great-great-grandma Ida made the most delicious collards, chicken, and make-you-dance biscuits," Honey said. "Her tea cakes were the best around."

"But those tea cakes were not for Grandma Ida's children or any other young slaves. They were never supposed to taste the cookies she baked.

"But some days Grandma Ida made a few extra, just the right size for hiding in her pocket. She risked being whipped to give the children a taste of sweet freedom.

butter

"Grandma Ida would give each child a tea cake," Honey said, "a promise of days to come." Tosh saw it all when Honey told her stories.

He loved their afternoons together. After Tosh finished his homework, he would help Honey set the table and she would give him the first taste of whatever was cooking in her cast-iron skillets.

sugar

Sometimes they sat on the porch and Tosh asked Honey to tell him the story of the tea cakes.

"Long ago," she always began.

Over time, Tosh didn't just imagine the journey, but he remembered the words just as Honey told him.

Then one day, things went wrong. Honey took them to the grocery store and forgot where she parked the car. They walked around and around until Tosh remembered where it was.

Another time, Honey held the phone in her hand and shook her head. "I've called my sister Elsie every day for the last fifty years. And now, for the life of me, I can't think of her number."

Tosh saw her phone book on top of a cabinet. "Is her number in here, Honey?" he asked, and gave it to her.

"Yes, baby. Thank you."

But the worst day was when Honey forgot how to make tea cakes. She just stared into the mixing bowl and said, "Hmmpf, just like that, it ran away from me."

"What ran away, Honey?" Tosh asked her.

"My mind, I guess," she said with a sigh. "I don't know what's wrong with your grandma today."

Tosh looked at Honey's worried face and checked all of the ingredients she placed on the counter—butter, flour, sugar, vanilla.

"What about eggs?" Tosh asked.

"Right, that's it," Honey said, beaming at Tosh. "You really are something."

flour

Honey seemed happy again, but she didn't tell Tosh the story of the tea cakes. When he asked her, she rested her head in her hand and said, "Grandma's a little too tired today."

When Mama came to pick up Tosh, he gave his grandma an extra hug good-bye.

baking powder

salt

cinnamon

Tosh asked Mama about Honey being so forgetful.
Mama kissed his head and said, "As some people grow older,
Tosh, their minds can have good spells and bad ones.
Some memories are clear as daylight. Others may turn hazy."

That evening, Tosh asked Mama to help him make tea cakes. He rolled the dough with a wooden pin. He cut the rounds with the floured rim of a glass and placed them on a greased cookie sheet with love.

When bedtime came, Tosh lay down and recited the story of the tea cakes until he fell asleep.

dough

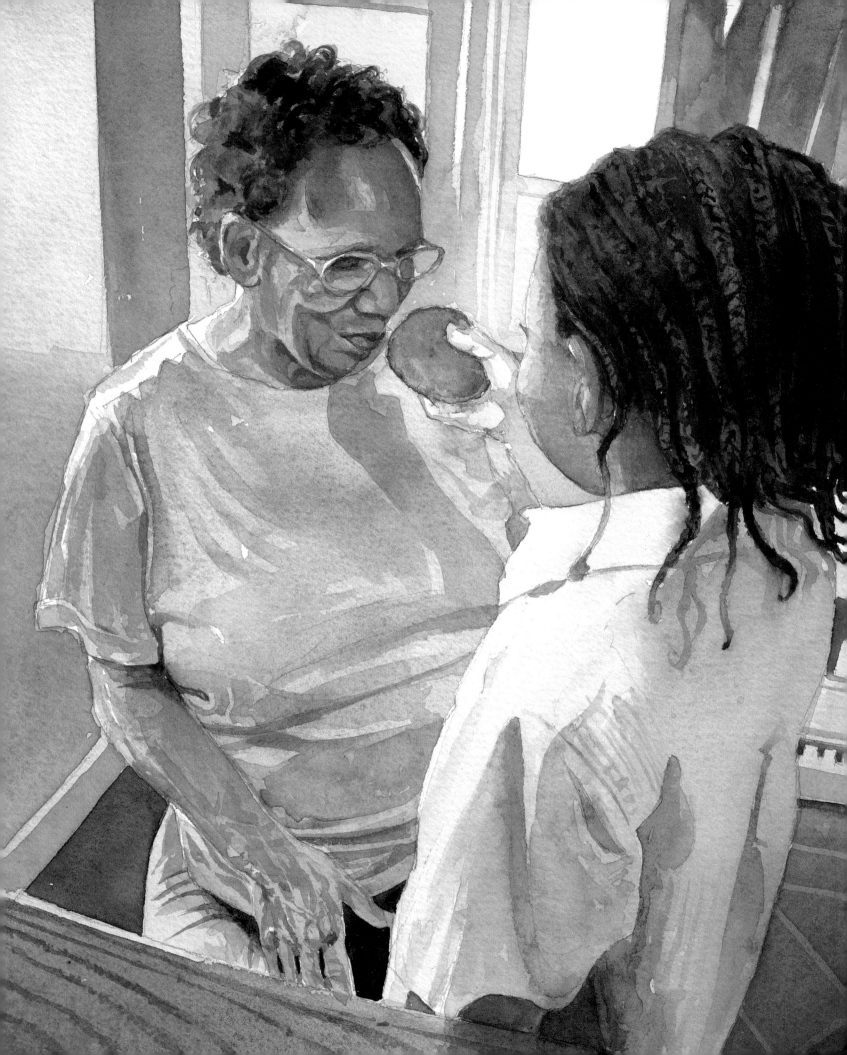

The next day, when he visited Honey, Tosh told her he had a surprise.

"Could you close your eyes, please?" he said.

Honey squeezed her eyes shut and Tosh put a tea cake to her lips. Honey smiled when she realized what it was.

"Long ago, before you and I were born," Tosh said, "our people were enslaved."

"Yes, baby," she said. "I can see it now."

tea cakes

In a blink, Tosh's words carried his grandma from her seat to the plantation, to a place neither had been but their hearts knew well.

They saw Grandma Ida and the golden cookies. They were there when she slid her hands into her pocket and a circle of young faces beamed with hope.

"And she gave each child a tea cake," Honey and Tosh said,
their words flying free, "a promise of days to come."

# Tea Cakes

2 sticks (1 cup) sweet cream butter

1¾ cup sugar, plus additional for
   topping

3 eggs, lightly beaten

1½ tsp. pure vanilla extract

3⅓ cups all-purpose flour

½ tsp. salt

1 tbsp. baking powder

Pinch of cinnamon, plus additional
   for topping

Rainbow sprinkles (optional)

Shortening (for lightly greasing
   cookie sheet)

Preheat oven to 350° F.

Cream softened butter and sugar. Mix in the eggs and vanilla until well blended and fluffy. Stir in flour mixed with next three ingredients. Mix thoroughly.

Lightly flour your hands so working with the dough is easier. Roll dough on a floured board, table or counter. Cut into circles or shapes with the floured rim of a glass or cookie cutter. Place on greased cookie sheet. Top with cinnamon sugar or rainbow sprinkles.

Bake until the cookies are set, about 12–14 minutes. Watch them carefully. Just the bottoms should brown. Cool and enjoy. Makes about two dozen cookies, depending on size.